James Daniel

And the

First Christmas

Wana T. Archer

Edited by Lauren Dykstra

Illustrations by Evyn Kron

ISBN-13:978-0615908168

ISBN-10:0615908160

Unless otherwise noted, all scripture quotations are from the Holy Bible, (KJV) King James Version. Language modernization is by the author.

DEDICATION

To James Daniel Dykstra
Inspiration for this Story

Son
Grandson
Great Grandson
Cousin
Nephew

"More is possible than we know."

About the Author

Dr. Wana Archer lives in Tulsa, Oklahoma, with his wife, Sammie. He is semi-retired after 47 years as a Baptist minister. He served congregations in Illinois, Ohio and Oklahoma.

Archer is a graduate of Southern Illinois University, Southwestern Baptist Theological Seminary, and Ohio State University, where he received the Ph.D. degree in adult education.

Author's Introduction

James Daniel and the First Christmas is historical
fiction. Characters and events drawn from the Bible are
as truthfully represented as the author's research could
possibly make them. Historical events based on
scripture are in chronological sequence.

The book was written to celebrate the birth of a first
great-grandchild, James Daniel Dykstra. It's the great-
grandparents' hope and prayer that James will grow up
giving thanks for his extended Christian family; and
also for a Savior whose birth is told with reverential
awe within these pages.

Contents

Prologue

The time was a long time ago. It was just before the time of the first Christmas.

In the faraway land of Israel a boy slept soundly on a bed of straw. He was asleep in the large barn of Elias, a livestock merchant to the city of Jerusalem. The sleeping boy was long and thin. His bare feet stretched beyond the wool mat that covered the straw. The boy's name was James Daniel.

He would be present for the first Christmas, although he didn't know it as he slept soundly on the bed of straw. This is his story and the story of the first Christmas.

Chapter 1
James Daniel

The large barn in which James Daniel slept was outside the massive wall that encircled Jerusalem. A house lay at the opposite end of the barn, separated by an enclosed yard and animal pens. It was on the busy south road that ran to Hebron.

The property belonged to Elias. The boy also belonged to Elias. James was a "born in the house" slave. His mother had been a foreign born slave purchased by a Jewish household. He had come to Elias, along with other property, as payment for a debt owed by his deceased master.

Elias had prepared a room and a bed for the boy in his modest home, but James Daniel chose to sleep in the barn. Elias accepted this with a simple shrug of his old shoulders.

James preferred the barn. He felt more comfortable in the company of animals. Animals were simple, honest creatures. People could be unkind and thoughtless. They had been unkind to the boy, especially when they learned that he was an orphan and a servant. There was one other thing: no one had ever heard the boy speak.

The old merchant was gruff and abrupt by nature, but kind to the boy. It was true that he owned James Daniel; but his ownership was an act of compassion, not cruelty. His intent was to protect the boy from the inhumanity of slavery. He had also been indentured for six years as a young man to settle a debt he couldn't pay.

The Judean sky lightened and warmed with the rising sun. The sleeping boy stirred and began to wake. In another barn, some 18 miles to the south near the city of Hebron, Jezebel slipped to her knees and then collapsed onto her side. Her final breath was a gentle sigh. She closed her eyes in an untroubled final rest. The quiet death of a little donkey named Jezebel would set James on the path to the first Christmas.

Chapter 2
Aaron and Rachel

The barn where Jezebel died belonged to Aaron the priest and his wife, Rachel. A yard separated the barn from a six-room house built of limestone blocks. Limestone was abundant in the area, and a favorite building material for those who could afford it. Most homes were simple four room structures made of large and small stacked stones, covered by a thatched roof

The house had been built by his great-grandfather, who had been a priest and a prosperous stonemason. It was near to Hebron, on the eastern side of the road. The road inclined upward from their home, to the plateau upon which the city of Hebron was built. It continued on to Beer Sheba and then to Egypt.

After the conquest of Canaan by the victorious Israelites, the land had been divided among the Twelve Tribes that had followed Moses out of Egyptian bondage. He had welded the separate tribes into the covenant people of God.

One tribe, the Tribe of Levi, was not given land because it was to be a tribe of priests and servants of God. They were to depend upon God for their living, *"because the Lord the God of Israel Himself is their inheritance."*

Instead, Joshua gave the Levites cities in which to dwell. The fabled General had designated Hebron as one of these cities. The Cave of Machpelah was there. It contained the remains of Abraham, Sarah, Isaac, Rebecca, Jacob and Leah. This burial place made Hebron the second most holy city in Israel.

Many of the priests who lived in Hebron served in the temple complex in Jerusalem. Aaron and his friend Zacharias were among those who served.

Elizabeth, the wife of Zacharias, could trace her lineage back to Aaron, the first high priest. Her family had been among the first settlers in the Judean hill country. She and Zacharias lived opposite Aaron and Rachel on the western side of the Hebron road.

Aaron and Zacharias belonged to the course of Abijah, one of the 24 courses of priests who served in the temple. Each course served for one week, from Sabbath noon to Sabbath noon, twice a year. All 24 courses served during the holy days of Israel. Because they were in the same course, Aaron and Zacharias traveled and lodged together during trips to Jerusalem.

While the men were away, Rachel and Elizabeth looked after one another. The two women were nearly the same age. They traveled to Hebron together each week for shopping and on the Sabbath for synagogue. They were often in one another's homes doing the daily and seasonal chores common to rural life. They also shared a personal sadness: they were both childless.

Chapter 3
Jezebel

Aaron had finished his morning prayers and was putting away the Isaiah scroll when the door opened. Rachel came in from the morning milking. She set the pitcher of warm goat's milk on the floor and leaned against the door frame.

"Jezebel is dead," she said. There were tears in her dark brown eyes and her lips were pressed tightly in sorrow. Aaron rose and crossed to his wife of 30 years and put his arm around her.

Rachel leaned her head against his chest. "Husband we can't do without Jezebel."

Rachel rode Jezebel daily to the open country to graze their small flock of sheep. She also used her for the weekly trips up to Hebron. Walking was out of the question because of her age.

Aaron held her gently. "Yes, you're right. I'll ask the neighbors to help me give the old girl a proper burial today. Then I'll find a boy to take the sheep to pasture until I return from Jerusalem."

"And why not a girl," Rachel asked?

"Perhaps it will be a girl," Aaron replied. "I'll make an early start for Jerusalem tomorrow and call on Elias. The merchant will find a replacement for Jezebel."

Aaron hoped the new donkey would be better behaved than Jezebel. He had her teeth marks on his upper left arm. The foot she had stepped on (more than once) still ached each time the weather changed.

He had named her Jezebel, because, as he said: "She loves to persecute the priests of God." Rachel laughed at that and declared Aaron unkind to one of God's simple creatures.

Jezebel had been a different animal around Rachel. Rachel's gentleness calmed the difficult beast. Jezebel loved Rachel and would do anything for her mistress. She even came to accept and obey Aaron. He was certain it was because; he too, belonged to Rachel.

.The other donkey in the barn Aaron had named Ahab. "Jezebel is like her namesake queen manipulating poor Ahab to her every whim."

"Yes," said Rachel, "But our Jezebel will guide Ahab to do good, not evil."

"We shall see what we shall see," Aaron replied.

Aaron used Ahab for the journeys to Jerusalem to serve in the temple complex. His priestly service in the temple was an honor and the primary source of income for them. The temple service required him to be away from his beloved Rachel several times each year.

The following morning, Aaron and Zacharias were able to join a group of pilgrims on their way to Jerusalem to worship at the temple. Rachel was relieved by this. There was danger from thieves for those who traveled alone to David's city.

Chapter 4
Two for One and a Boy

Elias' establishment was outside the south gate of the Jerusalem wall. It consisted of a modest home and a large barn separated by an extensive stockyard. A number of covered holding pens were located behind the yard, forming the back fence. The animals ready for sale were kept in these pens. Beyond the back fence stretched open country, where his young servant James Daniel shepherded the sheep to graze upon the sparse vegetation.

Aaron led Ahab off the road and into the barn of Elias, while Zacharias and the pilgrims continued on to Jerusalem. The old merchant and a boy were sorting and grooming sheep. Elias was noted for producing healthy sheep without physical flaws or blemishes. These were the kind of sheep destined for the sacrificial altar of the temple. Only such lambs could be offered to the God of Israel for the atonement of sins.

Elias looked up and acknowledged Aaron. "Is Rachel well," he asked?

Aaron smiled and nodded. Elias continued. "And how is sweet Jezebel? Is she still serving you?"

Aaron handed the reins of Ahab to Elias. "I want you to stable Ahab while I'm in Jerusalem. We also need a replacement for Jezebel."

"Ah, has she bitten her last priest?" asked Elias.

Aaron nodded. "Neighbors were happy to help me with the burial. Several had been targets of her temper in the past. Out of respect for Rachel they were silent, if not sorry, about the old girl's passing."

"Rachel wants another just like Jezebel," Aaron continued. "Surely there isn't another like her. The Lord wouldn't make two such animals."

Elias turned to the boy. "James, go fetch The Queen."

The boy went to one of the stalls and led out a female donkey. The donkey walked toward them head held high, long ears up, and prancing daintily on four white fetlocks and little black hooves.

Aaron walked around the donkey, inspecting the animal. He rubbed her side as if to confirm something. "Elias, I can't buy this animal. She's heavy with a foal."

"She's the best animal I have to sell to you," Elias said. "She's young and as sweet as Jezebel was not. I'm willing to give you The Queen and her foal, two for the price of one. Take The Queen."

Aaron shook his head. "And what would I do when she delivers? I'm a priest. I don't know about these things. And what would I do with a wild colt?"

"The colt will not be a problem," Elias said. "I'll send James Daniel home with you. He knows almost as much about donkeys as I do."

James shifted uneasily.

"He's served me well. He'll do the same for you. He'll deliver the foal and train the young colt for saddle and plow."

The boy's face was unreadable, but his muscles were tensing as he gripped the Queen's rope tightly. James had memories of mistreatment at the hands of others. Years of kindness by Elias hadn't completely erased the mental scars.

Now Elias was offering to send him away to a strange place in the company of this unknown priest. Why? What had he done?

"Take the Queen back to the stall and brush her down," Elias said. "We will finish with the sheep later. I have business to talk over with my friend Aaron."

James led The Queen away, back to her stall.

After the boy had gone, Aaron turned to Elias. "Elias, how long have we done business?" he asked.

Elias thought for a moment. "We've known each other at least 25 years."

"At least that long," said Aaron. "I've never known you to intentionally lose money, but you will on this sale. Also, you've never owned slaves, yet this boy is obviously a servant. And now you're putting him in my service indefinitely."

"No," said Elias, "I want you to take him permanently."

It took a moment for Aaron to grasp what he had just heard. Indeed, Elias had said, "permanently."

"Aaron, do you believe in the providence of God?" Elias asked. "I know you do. When you walked into the barn today it was as though God said, 'Elias, here is the answer to your prayer for James Daniel.'"

Aaron's confusion was increasing. "What do you mean? What prayer? I was talking to you about buying a donkey. Now you're talking to me about a boy."

"Please," interjected Elias, "hear me out. This boy is an orphan and he doesn't speak. He came to me in the settlement of a debt after his owner died. I didn't want to take him but what could I do? I don't have a heart of stone."

"He could have been sold to anyone," Elias continued. "Or worse, he might have been turned out into the streets to run with the other lost boys of Jerusalem, begging and stealing and into every kind of trouble. I thought he might have a kinsman who would take him, but he has no family; none."

"Aaron, I'm old." He tapped his chest. "There's something wrong here. I think that I'll be gathered to heaven soon. I'm not unhappy with the thought except for leaving James Daniel. There's no one to care for him after I'm gone. He's become the grandson I never had."

"I know you and Rachel are childless." (Elias said this with no intent to hurt Aaron.) He went on, "You and your sweet Rachel would be good to him, of that I'm certain. Will you make a place in your life and your home for James?"

Aaron was stunned. He had come for a donkey. Now he was being offered an orphaned slave boy who was mute.

There was only one thing to say to Elias and that was, "No!"

But when he looked into the old man's eyes something in his heart (not his head) stopped him.

"I won't give you an answer now," Aaron replied. "But I'll return before sunset with an answer."

He and Elias clasped hands and Aaron turned and walked out of the barn toward Jerusalem.

Within the hour, he was at the prayer garden of Gethsemane. He sat under the overspreading branches of an ancient olive tree. The wind was cool on his face as he prayed,

"Lord God, what answer shall I give to Elias? What is best for Rachel? What is best for the boy? Lord God, make your will clear to me." The words of a Psalm slipped into his mind:

As a father pities his children, even so God pities them who fear him, for he knows our frame that we are dust.

Aaron lay down, using his arm for a pillow. He thought of Rachel. He thought of her delight when she held a baby or watched children play. And he remembered her sorrow, hidden from all but him, as the years passed with no baby of her own; no child of her own at play.

If Rachel had had a son before she passed the age of childbearing, he might have been the age of this quiet boy being offered to him.

The sun was slipping below the surrounding hills when Aaron returned to the barn. The old merchant sat cleaning the wool from his brushes.

"Yes?" asked Elias.

"Yes," replied Aaron. "I finish my service in the temple in one week. I'll return for the boy and the donkey if you haven't changed your mind."

"And will you change yours?" asked the old merchant.

"No," said Aaron, "it's settled. Rachel and I will make a home for the boy. Only God knows what will come of this day's business."

"Yes, it's in God's hands," said Elias. He and Aaron walked into the yard: one walking upright, the other stooped and breathing heavily.

Meanwhile, James was exercising The Queen by walking her around the enclosure. She followed him without halter or rope. The little donkey pranced about with her head up and ears erect. Her hooves kicked up little puffs of dust with each step. They stopped when they reached Elias and Aaron.

"James, Aaron will return in one week," Elias advised. "Have his donkey watered, fed and saddled. Do also for The Queen. You and The Queen will go with Aaron to Hebron. Have all of your belongings packed and take provisions for the journey."

The boy turned and walked toward the barn, the donkey following. His face remained expressionless but his pulse raced with uncertainty and fear.

Later that same evening, the kind Elias sat down with James and explained about the new home with Aaron and Rachel. Elias said it was for the best. What James understood was that he really had no choice. He had to accept his fate and hope that Elias had been wise.

Aaron left the barn and hurried to enter the city before the gates closed for the night. One week later, James and Aaron would begin the trip to Hebron. Hebron was the next step in the boy's journey to the first Christmas.

Chapter 5
Zacharias

The priests were freshly bathed and had put on ceremonial clothing for the temple service. Each wore linen trousers that reached below their knees. The garment was worn next to the body for the sake of modesty.

The outer garment for temple priests was a white linen tunic. It was gathered about the waist by a 5-inch linen sash embroidered with fine blue, purple, and scarlet threads.

The final piece was a linen headband that symbolized humility before God.

Each priest was barefoot. The Lord had spoken from the burning bush to Moses saying,

"Take off your shoes. The ground upon which you are standing is holy ground."

Therefore whatever the weather, the priests wore no shoes out of reverence for the sacred temple.

The morning sky was still gray as the priests crossed the great court and paused before the gate to the temple enclosure. Only priests were permitted within the gate.

The gate opened and each priest went immediately to his appointed task in silence.

Aaron climbed the steps to the large brass altar just inside the enclosure. He scraped the ashes from the altar and allowed them to fall through the grates in the floor. He heaped the coals from the evening sacrificial fire into a mound. Kindling was added and caught immediately. More wood was added. The fire burned hot with coals glowing red.

Zacharias was appointed to serve at the altar of incense in the holy place of the temple. He approached the sacrificial altar with the golden censer that would be placed within the inner altar of incense. He positioned the censer on the step near Aaron. Aaron used tongs to pluck flaming coals from the altar and deposit them into the censer.

Zacharias picked up the golden censer and carried it to the door of the temple. He waited nervously for the door to open. Priests were selected to serve in the temple by lot. It would perhaps be the only time he would enter the holy place of the sanctuary in his lifetime.

A priest opened the door and Zacharias stepped inside. The door closed behind him. He was alone in the sanctuary of God. He looked about, drinking in the beauty of the ornate wood and inlaid gold of the walls and ceiling.

It was a windowless room, 30 feet in length and 15 feet in width. A large, multi-layered veil hung at the back of the room. The rich tapestry was decorated with the images of two lions and an eagle. It separated the holy place from the room called the holy of holies. Only the high priest entered this most sacred room, and then only on the Day of Atonement.

The golden lampstand symbolizing the light of God was on the left side of the room, directly opposite the table of showbread. The lampstand was of solid gold. It was shaped like an almond branch and consisted of a base, stem and lights.

Three branches rose out of the two sides of the stem. The six branches and the stem were each topped by a cup in the shape of an almond blossom. A bowl for oil rested in each cup.

The seven bowls had been filled with the finest olive oil. The linen wicks were trimmed and lit. The seven lamps filled the room with a soft glow.

To the right of Zacharias was the table of showbread. The small table was 3 feet long and half as wide. It was made of acacia wood overlaid with gold.

Twelve loaves of flat, unleavened bread, made from the finest flour, were stacked on the table. The loaves remained on the table until the following Sabbath. Then the priests were required to eat the bread within the holy place. Twelve fresh loaves were placed on the table until the next Sabbath.

The bread represented the twelve tribes of Israel which were always in the presence of the Lord.

The golden altar of incense was directly in front of the temple curtain that separated the holy place and the holy of holies. This rectangular inner altar was made of hard, close grained shittim wood covered in pure gold. The altar stood three feet in height with an 18 inch inner chamber for the golden censer.

Zacharias moved to the altar and placed the golden censer of hot coals within it. He then added incense to the hot coals. Smoke with a fragrant odor began to rise up into the room.

Zacharias knelt and began his prayers of adoration, praise and intercession. He exalted and gave thanks for the thrice holy God of Israel. He prayed for the consolation of Israel under the heel of Rome, and the cruelty of Herod the King.

And then Zacharias prayed for his dear Elizabeth and the burden of her barrenness. He would be unprepared for Heaven's answer.

Chapter 6
Gabriel

Zacharias rose to his feet and looked about the holy place of the temple. A golden haze filled every part of it. The gold of the ceiling and walls shimmered in the light. A halo encircled each of the seven lamps on the golden stand.

Zacharias turned back to the altar of incense. A radiant white figure, haloed by the light, stood on the right side of the altar. When Zacharias saw the angel he gasped and stepped back.

But the angel said to him; "Don't be afraid, Zacharias: for the prayer you and Elizabeth have been praying for a long time has been heard. Elizabeth is going to have a son, and you are to name him John. This shall be an occasion of great joy and your home will overflow with gladness."

Zacharias shook his head from side to side in disbelief. "This can't be," he said. "We're too old. We couldn't possibly have a child now."

The glowing white figure beside the altar spoke again: "I am Gabriel, the angel who stands in the presence of the Lord. I was sent to give you this good news. Your son is going to be the one who will announce the coming of the long-promised Christ."

Zacharias absorbed the words of the angelic being. He and Elizabeth were to be the parents of the prophesied forerunner that would prepare the way for Israel's promised Messiah! Once again, he shook his head in disbelief.

The shimmering white figure seemed to grow larger. "Because you won't believe me, you will not be able to speak until the baby is born." Then, the angel vanished from beside the golden altar.

Zacharias searched the room. It was empty and silent. He sank again to his knees in prayer. His doubts vanished and were replaced by a sense of joy, just as angel Gabriel had said.

Zacharias rushed out of the temple, past the altar of sacrifice and the startled Aaron. He ran into the great court outside the temple gate. A large number of men had gathered there to worship. Many women were also in the upper court. He gestured and pointed, but he couldn't speak. Someone in the crowd of men said, "He's seen a vision of God!" There was an audible murmur in the upper and lower courts.

That evening, Zacharias wrote out an account of what had happened in the holy place, and gave it to his friend. Aaron read it and was astonished by the story.

He and Zacharias belonged to the religious order of Sadducees. Sadducees didn't believe in angels. They didn't believe in the immortal soul or life after death. Sadducees were convinced that God rewarded and punished persons in the here-and-now, and not in the hereafter.

But Zacharias was claiming that an angel had spoken to him in the holy place. Either he was mistaken or the Sadducees were wrong. And if they were wrong about angels, what else?

The other priests didn't know what to make of Zacharias and his sudden silence. He became the object of their furtive glances and whispered conversations.

. . .

The angel Gabriel had disappeared from Zacharias and the temple, to later reappear in Nazareth of Galilee to a young woman named Mary. Gabriel would announce to Mary that she had been chosen to be the mother of the son of God.

The first Christmas was coming to the world.

Chapter 7
Leaving Elias

23 And it came to pass, that, as soon as the days of his ministration were accomplished, he (Zacharias) departed to his own house.
Luke 1:23

When the term ended Zacharias and Aaron left Jerusalem as soon as the south gate was opened. They arrived at Elias' barn at first light. The old merchant and the boy were already in the yard preparing the donkeys for the journey.

The boy was dressed like a young David tending his sheep on a Judean hillside. His head was covered with a linen head piece reaching to his shoulders. It was held in place by a narrow strip of embroidered cloth. His tunic was also of linen cloth. The garment left his arms and shoulders uncovered and free for movement. It descended to the knees.

He wore a leather belt with a leather pouch on the left side. His sling and two smooth round stones were in the pouch. A knapsack of heavy wool cloth containing his personal belongings was slung across his shoulder. His feet were shod with sturdy, thick-soled sandals.

The boy held a shepherd's staff with a crooked handle. He used it as a walking stick over the rocky, uneven Judean countryside. The shepherd's rod with its rounded head and leather wrist strap was secured to the right side of the leather belt about his waist.

The rod was 18 inches of hard seasoned wood; the same length as a Roman soldier's short sword. James used it to push the sheep away from poisonous plants and onto safe trails. He would also throw it to drive unwary sheep away from danger. Its effectiveness depended on the skill and practice of the individual. James was very good with it.

James could also use it much like a sword to thrust and strike at any attacker. Fortunately, he had never had to use it to strike a wild beast or a human.

Elias slowly straightened to greet Aaron.

He handed him a scroll. "This is testimony that today I release James Daniel from servitude to me. I grant him ownership of all his personal effects. And I award him a monetary sum for the five years he has served me. Hold it in keeping for him. He will serve you until he comes of age, then he is free."

Elias stepped closer to James Daniel and placed his hands on the boy's shoulders. The boy had grown taller than the old man. "Do you understand what I have just done?" James nodded.

Then, the old man put his arms around the stoic boy and gently embraced him. "Go with God," he said gruffly.

James Daniel looked around at the surroundings that had been his home for five years. He looked at the old man who had been kind and bowed his head to Elias. Then he turned and led Ahab and The Queen across the yard, to the open gate and the road to Hebron.

Chapter 8
Journey to Hebron

The road to Hebron dipped and rose between sandy, rocky hills and arid countryside. Aaron and Zacharias walked more than they rode. James studied the two priests. Aaron talked but Zacharias only nodded. Sometimes he didn't seem to hear Aaron and stared into the distance.

James Daniel also walked, leading The Queen with a loose rope about her neck. He carried his knapsack to lighten her burden.

The road narrowed and clung tenaciously to a rocky hillside. It was here that three men rushed from a covering of rocks and attacked the little group. Two of the thieves pushed Aaron and Zacharias to the ground and stood over them with raised clubs.

The third thief saw movement out of the corner of his eye. He saw the jerk of the boy's arm as the stone was released from the sling. He never saw the round stone even after it glanced off of the bridge of his nose. He sank to his knees, crying in pain and covering his face with his hands.

The other two thieves looked at their companion on the ground and then at James. They rushed at the boy with a shout of anger.

James slipped around to the other side of The Queen and knelt down. As the two thieves rushed by the side of The Queen, James slipped the crooked end of the shepherd's staff under the belly of the animal. The boy snared the ankle of the first thief. The man fell into the dust of the road, tripping the second thief, who tumbled on top of him.

The thief jumped up and rushed around The Queen to get at the boy. As he passed behind the donkey, James Daniel reached up and tickled her underbelly. Small black hooves shot out and struck the thief on the knee. He sank to the ground howling and grabbing his knee. James tickled the belly of The Queen again, and again little black hooves flashed, striking the kneeling thief on the chin. He slumped silently onto his back.

The second thief had now scrambled to his feet. He reached across the back of the Queen to grab James. Instead, he felt the blunt end of the staff against his chest. The boy heaved upward, levering his strength behind the staff. The thief propelled backward to the edge of the road. The loose rocks and earth gave way and he slid off the road and down the side of the hill. The downward slide was stopped abruptly by a large boulder. The thief lay still.

James stood up and slipped the staff onto the saddle pack. He grabbed the rounded head of the shepherd's rod and pulled it from his belt at the ready. Then he put his arm around The Queen to calm her.

Aaron had gotten to his feet in time to witness the impromptu battle. He looked at the boy calmly stroking The Queen's ears, shepherd's rod drawn.

He looked to heaven and said with amazement, "Have you sent me a young David bringing down Goliath, or a young Samson slaying the Philistines with the hooves of a donkey?"

The thieves were gathered up and made to sit on the side of the road. The one who had been hit by the glancing stone was nursing his bruised nose. The other two sat dazed and covered with dust.

Aaron demanded answers from the humbled thieves. "Why are you falling upon innocent strangers to rob them?"

The one holding his nose said, "We were hungry and desperate. That's why we tried to rob you. We never meant to harm you. We were only going to take a little silver, that's all."

"Who are you?"

"I'm Eliphaz," the spokesman said. "These are my brothers, Bildad and Zophar."

Aaron actually laughed out loud upon hearing the names of the bumbling trio.

"Our names are from the scroll of Job," Eliphaz continued. "You being a priest would know that."

"We're farmers and shepherds. We lived on a small farm with our father. He died, and the soldiers came and took our farm to pay taxes to Rome and King Herod. Since that time, we have wandered from place to place, looking for work and finding none. Our hunger made us desperate."

Aaron believed him because the story was all too common in Israel. He felt pity for the ragged brothers and called for James to bring food and water for them. As James served them they watched the boy with respectful admiration.

James treated their wounds with a balm made from the oils of the olive and commiphora trees. Elias had taught him how to harvest the resin, called myrrh, and combine it with olive oil into an antiseptic paste. The brothers thanked him and he returned to stand beside The Queen.

Aaron gave each of the men a small silver coin. He also gave them the name of a landowner near Bethlehem who might offer jobs to them. Aaron thought the song of Moses would be an appropriate farewell for the vanquished brothers.

He knelt in prayer, and the brothers bowed their heads:

"The Lord is our strength and song.
And he is become our salvation.
He is our God.

We will prepare him a habitation,
the God of our fathers,
and exalt him."

"Amen," said Aaron. "Amen," said the brothers.

The little party moved on toward Hebron, while the brothers limped back toward Bethlehem. They talked among themselves about the kindness of the priests and their new hope for work.

They also spoke about the strange, silent youth who had vanquished them. James Daniel and the brothers would meet again. It would be on the night of the first Christmas.

Chapter 9
Coming Home

24 And after those days his wife Elisabeth conceived, and hid herself five months, saying, 25 "Thus has the Lord dealt with me in the days wherein he looked on me, to take away my reproach among men."
Luke 1:24-25

Aaron brought Zacharias into the house, where Elizabeth greeted him with a kiss. James Daniel waited at the door, watching and listening.

"Zacharias has had a shock, Elizabeth. He can't speak." Aaron handed her the parchment that told of the angel's appearance in the sanctuary.

She read it and looked at Zacharias. "The angel of the Lord said we're to have a child? Is this true?" she asked.

Zacharias nodded. Elizabeth moved into his beckoning arms and he held her as she wept softly.

Aaron and James slipped out of the house and crossed the road to the limestone house and Rachel.

Aaron handed the reins of Ahab to James, and said: "Take Ahab and the Queen to the barn. After you have cared for them, I want you to come to the house to meet Rachel. "

James led the donkeys into the barn. It was almost as large as the house. A small flock of sheep had already been penned up for the night. The goat slept contentedly in her pen.

He fed and watered the donkeys and checked and cleaned their hooves. Then he brushed the road dust from their reddish coats. Lastly, he spread fresh hay in the stalls. The weary animals sank onto their knees in the fresh straw and were quickly asleep.

The saddle packs, bits, and ropes he stored in the room where the farm implements were kept. James chose that room for himself. He placed his knapsack on a table in the room and spread hay in one corner. He rolled out the wool mat onto the fresh hay. A small window in the corner of the room opened to let in the cool night air. He would be able to see the stars from his bed.

The boy washed his face and hands and pushed the hair back from his forehead. He ran his fingers through his brown hair to untangle and smooth it. He crossed the yard separating the barn and the house.

When James Daniel entered the house, Rachel came to meet him.

"Aaron has told me about you," she said. "I'm happy he brought you here. You were so brave against the thieves. This is your home now."

She embraced him and placed a soft kiss on each cheek. A memory from the shadowy past rose up and took hold of James. He was small and a woman held him gently against her breast. She sang as she rocked him to sleep. The images in the memory were faded, except for the voice.

Rachel stepped away. He seemed not to see her for a moment. Then he focused on her large brown eyes and soft smile. He acknowledged her graciousness by bowing his head. She invited him to the table and the evening meal began.

James listened as Aaron told Rachel of the appearance of the angel to Zacharias in the temple. He told her of the baby that Elizabeth was to have in her old age. "The baby is to announce the coming of the promised Christ," he said.

Rachel said, "Oh Aaron, can it be that we will live to see the consolation of Israel?"

Aaron reached across the table and took the hand of his wife. "It's difficult to believe that an angel appeared in the temple and actually spoke to Zacharias. I'm certain he believes it. Something did happen to him. In time we will know the truth. The angel promised a miracle, and perhaps it will come to pass."

After supper, Aaron told James Daniel to return to the barn and bring his belongings to the house for the night. The boy left the house. Time passed and he didn't return.

A concerned Rachel asked, "Why hasn't he returned?"

"I don't believe he's coming," Aaron replied. "He's chosen to sleep in the barn with the animals. It was his way with old Elias. It will be his way with us. I think he finds a comfort with the simple creatures that is lacking with people. In time it may be different. Let's be patient with the boy for now."

James Daniel sat on his bed of straw and gazed at the stars through the little window. He drew the reed pipe from his knapsack and placed it to his lips. He began to play the lullaby the woman of his memory had sung to him:

> *God gives sleep my little one.*
> *Now steals upon my sleepy one.*
> *Sleep on, sleep on, and sleep on.*
>
> *Go to sleep, my little one.*
> *Sleepy eyes close, my little one.*
> *Sleep on, sleep on, and sleep on.*
>
> *Angels watch o'er my little one,*
> *Love enfolds my little one.*
> *Sleep on, sleep on, and sleep on.*
>
> *Go to sleep, my little one.*
> *Sleepy eyes close, my little one.*
> *Sleep on, sleep on, and sleep on.*

The boy stretched his thin, weary body on the soft bed of straw. His eyes closed and he slept the untroubled sleep of the young.

Chapter 10
Little Prince

Noises from The Queen's stall awakened James. He lit a lamp and peered into the stall. The Queen lay on her side. She was delivering her foal. The sounds were the painful cries of a difficult birth.

He went to the donkey and examined her. This was The Queen's first foal, and the colt was large. She would need help if she and the foal were to survive the birth.

James crossed the yard to the house and knocked at the door. It was Rachel who opened to him. He pointed at the barn and made a circle of his arms in front of his stomach. He pushed downward with his hands. Rachel understood immediately that a birth was happening. The door closed and the boy returned quickly to the barn and The Queen.

He found a length of rope in the tack room and tied a slip knot at one end. He returned to the stall and The Queen with the rope. He searched for the position of the foal. The loop of rope was slipped around the forequarters of the foal and drawn tight.

An excited and breathless Rachel appeared. She had run across the yard to the barn. She gave James a smile. "What can I do?" she asked.

He handed the rope end to her and returned to the Queen to position the foal. Rachel pulled on the rope, drawing out the foal as James guided the forequarters and the head. As the Queen pushed, Rachel pulled and

James added his strength. The colt was delivered safely onto the hay of the stall.

Rachel looked at the shiny wet colt resting in the straw. "The Queen has a little prince," she said happily. "Prince will be his name."

Then she laughed and said, "What will the neighbors say about Aaron and Rachel? Now we have three donkeys. One named for a king. One called The Queen and now a Prince! Has any household ever celebrated such lowly creatures?"

Then she was gone out of the barn to the house to tell Aaron about the birth of the colt named Prince.

James wiped down the little Prince with straw. He helped The Queen to rise and guided the newborn to her milk. That is how he left them as he returned to his bed where sleep returned quickly.

Chapter 11
Milk Maid

The light of the morning sun had not reached the yard when Rachel crossed it to the barn. She noticed that the sheep were in the outer pen and had already been watered.

She entered the barn for the morning milking. The goat was already tethered to the milking post and the milking stool was in place. Hay and grain were already in the feeding trough. The goat munched contentedly.

James was mucking out the sheep pen and spreading fresh hay. Rachel sat on the stool and began the morning milking.

"Thank you for having everything ready this morning," Rachel said. "After breakfast please saddle Ahab for me. We will drive the sheep to the open country. I'll accompany you until you learn your way. Aaron wishes you to join him in the house when you have finished here."

James entered the house to find Aaron studying one of his many scrolls of scripture. He motioned for the boy to sit down opposite him.

"I want you to join me each morning after chores," Aaron instructed. "Time will be spent in scripture study before you take the sheep to pasture."

He handed the boy a rectangular shard of limestone painted in black and framed in wood. A verse was printed on it.

"Each evening after supper, I will erase the verse on the tablet. You must print it from memory."

James nodded.

"The exception is the Sabbath. Sabbath is for synagogue and rest from our labors, as did the Lord God on the seventh day."

Again, the boy nodded.

James looked at the verse on the table:

Your word have I hid in my heart, that I might not sin against you.

Thus, the pattern of the boy's new life was established in the home of Aaron and Rachel. James had always been comfortable with work and routine, but scripture study was new. He proved to have a good mind for it.

After breakfast, James saddled Ahab for Rachel. They released the sheep from the pen and drove them out into the open country. As they passed through the open country, Rachel would draw directions on the ground to point out the best sources of water and grazing.

This first morning the sheep were driven to a favorite meadow. A stream flowed from a mountain spring, forming a pool of cold, clear water at the lowest point of the stream. Other flocks were already grazing when they arrived.

A girl was there watching over a small herd of goats. She sat on a rock that protruded from the hillside.

Rachel went over to her, embraced her and sat beside her on the rock.

"Jemania, this is James Daniel. He will be caring for our sheep."

The girl bowed her head to the boy. Her dark eyes studied his face.

"This is Jema's favorite place," Rachel said. "She thinks this is her rock. Her name is even carved on it."

The girl laughed and pointed to the side of the rock. There were the letters, JEMA.

"She's our little milk maid," Rachel continued. "Her father is a milk and cheese merchant to Hebron. They also live on the Hebron road. As our neighbors, I want you to watch out for her and help her."

"And as a good neighbor I'll watch out for you James Daniel." Jema said this with a little grin that turned up the corners of her mouth. She watched the boy's face. James nodded but his expression didn't change.

This girl could not have imagined the impact she was having on the tall, thin boy with the brown hair and blue eyes.

Nor could James have explained it to anyone. Something wonderfully new was happening inside of him as he watched her.

She wore a head covering that reached to her shoulders. It was held in place by a gaily decorated head band tied behind her small head. Two long braids of luxurious black hair swept from beneath the covering and lay upon her young breast.

A fine linen dress covered her from neck to feet. The arms were also covered to the wrists. It was embroidered at the neck, wrists and hem. A cloth belt gathered it at her waist. Her feet were drawn up beneath the hem.

The eyes that studied James were dark pools framed by long, black lashes. Dark expressive eyebrows arched over her eyes. Her nose was straight and slender. Her soft lips and mouth curved upward ever so slightly at the corners, giving her a constant expression of delight.

James had never seen or heard anything quite like her. He had to force himself to look away from her.

Rachel and the girl had brought sewing material. They talked and sewed. James used the time and the abundance of smooth, round stones to practice his sling. The girl would occasionally look up from her sewing to watch the stones fly at distance targets.

At noon, Rachel said: "We will move the sheep and goats to water and find shade for our lunch."

Jema stood up and the dress rose to her ankles. It uncovered one small, perfectly formed and sandaled foot. The other foot was wrapped in cloth strips. It turned inward and was twisted with deformity.

She picked up a walking stick beside the rock and fitted it under her arm. Next, she looked at the boy defiantly. She searched his face for some sign of contempt. His eyes looked at her steadily, unchanging.

He turned, still looking at her, and stumbled over his feet. He regained his balance. He looked back over his shoulder and she was smiling. His face grew strangely warm. He herded the sheep and goats toward the water.

The boy quickly gained the same measure of trust with Rachel that he had earned with Aaron on the journey to Hebron. After only a few days, she stopped coming with James.

Jema welcomed his silent company when he brought the sheep to graze near her. She would sew and sing. He would study his limestone tablet.

They shared their lunches. Afterward, Jema would lie back to rest, tucking the hem of her dress over her small twisted foot. The boy would play songs on his reed pipe. Jema sang or hummed the songs familiar to her. Her favorite was one taken from the Song of Songs:

Rose of Sharon:
Lily of the Valley.
Apple tree among trees:
Apricots ripe with fragrance.

So is my beloved among the sons.
Under his shadow, I will delight.
Love of my beloved:
Fruit sweet to taste.

The months passed in a pleasant rhythm of sameness. A small herd of goats and a small herd of sheep often grazed together. A silent young shepherd and a dark eyed milk maid sat near to each other.

Then a young woman named Mary arrived in the home of Zacharias and Elizabeth. She was on a journey to the first Christmas. James would be caught up and carried away from Jema by Mary's journey.

Chapter 12
Mary

A few days after Mary's arrival, Rachel told James and Aaron about the guest at the home of Zacharias and Elizabeth.

They had just finished the evening meal and James started to rise. He felt Rachel's hand on his, and he sat back down.

Rachel said, "Zacharias and Elizabeth have a visitor. It's a young woman from Nazareth of Galilee. Her name is Mary, and she is Elizabeth's cousin."

Aaron thought of the distance between Hebron and Nazareth. The young woman had traveled from one end of Israel to the other. "Why would she undertake such a long journey?" he asked.

"The angel Gabriel told her that Elizabeth was expecting a child," Rachel explained. "I believe she's come to help and encourage Elizabeth."

"That was the name of the angel Zacharias saw in the temple," Aaron said with growing interest. "The angel's message was true. Elizabeth is expecting a child in her old age. But still, why would the angel tell this young woman?"

Rachel became very animated with her next bit of news. "The angel also prophesied to Mary that she would have a child. The child will be the son of God and the promised Christ! Mary is a virgin and has no husband, yet she is expecting a child."

"Wife, we both know that a virgin isn't going to be expecting a child," Aaron said quietly.

Rachel disagreed. "I think it's a miracle, just as Elizabeth's baby is a miracle. Elizabeth is convinced it's true. She believes the lives of the two babies are intertwined. She said she experienced great joy, as did the baby in her womb, when Mary entered her home. She is convinced Mary's child is the Christ."

Aaron shook his head. "The Christ couldn't possibly be born to a young woman from Galilee. Surely Jerusalem will be the place of his birth, perhaps in a palace."

"Why must he be born in a palace?" asked Rachel. "Was King David born in a palace? And isn't the Christ a descendent of King David?"

While Aaron and Rachel were talking, James was printing on his tablet. He handed the tablet to Aaron. Aaron read the inscription and then passed it to Rachel. The boy had printed:

Therefore the Lord himself shall give you a sign; Behold, a virgin shall conceive, and bear a son, and shall call his name Immanuel.

"It's one of the verses that James has memorized from the Isaiah scroll," Aaron said. "Still, it's hard to believe that the prophecy is being fulfilled in this young woman from Galilee."

Rachel's voice was solemn. "I have met Mary and have spoken with her. You too, will believe when you meet her."

The boy took the tablet and erased the words. He began to print again. He handed the tablet to Aaron. Aaron read out loud:

"But you, Bethlehem Ephratah, though you are small among thousands of Judah, yet out of you shall come forth to me a ruler in Israel; whose origins have been from of old, from everlasting."

Aaron turned to the boy. "Yes James, it's a prophecy from the prophet Micah. But, it's a mystery. How is it possible for a new king to come from such an obscure village as Bethlehem?"

Aaron and Rachel continued the discussion as she cleared the dishes from the table. Aaron brought the Isaiah scroll from its cherished cabinet and spread it on the table. Then he and Rachel searched it to find and read the passages that told of the coming Christ.

James Daniel left the limestone house and returned to the barn. He sat on his bed of straw. The moon and evening star were visible through the small window. He began to play his reed pipe:

The heavens are the work of your fingers.
The moon and stars you have ordained.
O Lord, how excellent is your name in all the earth.

Praise him sun and moon.
Praise him all you stars of light.
O Lord, how excellent is your name in all the earth.

He put aside the pipe and lay back to stare up into the darkness. The dark eyes of Jema looked back at him. Then, he was asleep.

Chapter 13
Leaving Hebron

41 And it came to pass, that, when Elisabeth heard the salutation of Mary, the babe leaped in her womb. And Elisabeth was filled with the Holy Spirit: 42 and she spoke out with a loud voice, and said, "Blessed are you among women, and blessed is the fruit of your womb."
Luke 1:41-42

Zacharias watched two mysteries unfold beneath the thatched roof of his home beside the Hebron road. The first was the miracle promised by the angel Gabriel. He and Elizabeth would soon be parents. The second was the divine mystery of godliness that was being fulfilled in Mary. The growing life she carried within would be fully human, yet also fully divine.

Then Mary quite suddenly decided to end her visit before the birth of Elizabeth's child. Elizabeth understood.

Mary no longer acted according to time or circumstance. The hand of God guided her in everything she did. It had been so ever since she had said to the angel Gabriel, "I am the handmaid of the Lord."

This imminent departure of Mary sent Elizabeth and Zacharias across the Hebron road to see their friends.

Elizabeth explained the reason for their visit. "Mary is returning home. Zacharias and I believe she shouldn't undertake this long journey alone. He has great confidence in James." Zacharias nodded agreement. "We're asking that he travel with her to Nazareth."

This surprised Aaron and Rachel. Rachel spoke first: "It's a long way to Galilee. Once there how would he come back to us?" Her voice became urgent. "He must come back."

Elizabeth had anticipated this. "Next year, large numbers of people will travel from Galilee to Judea for the census ordered by Rome," she explained. "James could return safely with some of them."

The four adults turned to the boy. Aaron said, "They're asking you to go with Mary to Nazareth. You would look after her and protect her. You would be away from us for a long time. Do you want to do this?"

James thought of Mary and the baby. Nothing must harm them. If God had a part for him, he would fulfill it. Yes, he would go. He nodded.

Elizabeth suddenly realized she had been holding her breath waiting for the response. She breathed out in relief. "Thank you, James. God will bless you for this."

. . .

As Elizabeth and Zacharias crossed back over the Hebron road, they began to discuss what Mary should take on the journey. Meanwhile, James, tablet in hand, left the house and went immediately to the barn. He sat down and began to write on the tablet. When he had finished, he walked to Jema's home.

. . .

Jema and her mother answered his knock. The mother smiled at the tall thin boy. Jema was surprised to see him in the evening. "What is it James?" She asked. He handed her the tablet on which he had written:

I am going away. You may use this. I will return for it.

The mother put her arm around the shoulders of her daughter. They both understood the unwritten thought beneath the message on the tablet. James was giving a pledge to Jema. Her dark eyes softened and moistened. She pressed her lips together to hold back the tears.

"I promise to keep the tablet for you until you return," Jema said with trembling voice. She and her mother bowed to the boy who stood silently on the doorstep.

James bowed his head to the mother and daughter. Then he turned and walked away down the Hebron road. He entered the barn and began preparation for the journey. He had decided to take The Queen to Nazareth.

Chapter 14
Suki

56 And Mary stayed with her (Elizabeth) about three months, and returned to her own home.
Luke 1:56

The trip to Jerusalem began at sunrise. Mary and James paused in a small village at noontime for food and rest. James watered and fed the animals before setting off again. By late afternoon, Jerusalem could be seen in the distance.

They could also see smoke rising from a deep ravine just ahead. The ravine, also called Gehenna, began near the Jerusalem wall. It ran parallel to the road for some distance before turning east. It smoldered with fires fed by the refuse of Jerusalem.

Gehenna was a synonym for evil to many in Israel. The pre-Israelite population had used the valley as a place of infant and child sacrifice to idol gods. The unclaimed bodies of the homeless and the criminal had also been dumped into the ravine's unquenched fires.

Wild dogs lived around the ravine and fed off of the refuse dumped there.

Elias had instructed James to stay clear of the ravine when grazing sheep in the open country. He had also told James of the natural enmity between donkeys and wild dogs.

Elias had warned: "Ride away from these dogs if you can. Whatever you do, stay mounted."

James pointed to Mary's donkey. Then, he mounted the back of The Queen. Mary understood and mounted her donkey. James handed her his shepherd's rod. The rod was an extension of the shepherd's arm. A leather strap secured it to the hand and wrist. Mary slipped the strap onto her wrist and gripped the rounded head.

The little party advanced down the road, beside the ravine. The yelping of the scavenger dogs drifted up from Gehenna. Just then, an ugly, gaunt beast of a dog came up out of the ravine, followed by 10 other large, filthy curs. A ravenous hunger united the animals. Their hunger had given them the boldness to seek prey on the road.

James and Mary stopped. The little party backed away, but the dogs advanced toward them.

The dogs snarled and growled and snapped at one another, working themselves into a rage. They lowered their bodies; muscles coiled and fangs exposed, ready to spring upon the travelers.

Further retreat was impossible. The Queen lowered her head and pawed the ground, sending little clouds of dust into the air. James touched her flanks with his heels and she charged the dogs.

They were quickly into the snarling beasts. James wielded his shepherd's staff to the left and right, delivering painful blows to the attacking dogs.

The pack leader gaped and bit at James' exposed leg. He thrust the staff like a sword, striking the vicious beast between the eyes. The dog fell back to the ground and was stepped on by the Queen's hard, black hoof.

The Queen snapped and kicked at the attacking curs. One of them bit into her fetlock, but was sent tumbling off of the road. Her hooves stomped and kicked. The dogs howled in pain and backed away.

Once through the dogs, James and The Queen wheeled about and charged them again. The half-starved, cowardly animals had no time to regroup. They fled before The Queen and James, running back down into the ravine to get away from her powerful hooves and his painful blows.

Mary had watched the battle, ready to ride into the fray to help. Now she moved forward to join James and The Queen.

A series of little yelps drew their attention to a pup that had climbed up out of the ravine, too late for the attack. The gangly, malnourished little animal bravely charged them anyway.

The Queen stepped forward to meet the charge. The pup saw The Queen and skidded, somersaulting on to the dusty road. It landed beneath The Queen's nose. She smelled the little animal and snorted. The little dog scrambled backward and tumbled again. It lay in the road weak and gaunt from hunger.

James walked to the limp and dirty little dog and scooped it up. He held it up for the young woman to see. Then he walked to the edge of the road ready to send the pup back down into the ravine. The pup raised its head and looked at James out of large eyes above a narrow muzzle.

James hesitated, his hands frozen in midair over the edge of the ravine. He studied the small sad creature, turning it from side to side. Beneath the dirt the dog was a tri-color of black, white and tan. The ears were soft and long beside its narrow head and large eyes. Its body held a promise of lean grace.

James turned away from the ravine and carried the dog back to the donkeys. An empty knapsack was hung on The Queen's saddle pack. He placed the pup in the bag, and it fell asleep immediately from exhaustion.

The group traveled safely beyond the ravine before stopping again. There were streaks of blood on The Queen's legs and some of it was her own. James cleaned and treated her minor cuts with the antiseptic salve. He rubbed some of the myrrh and olive oil paste into the cuts on his own legs. Then he gave the Queen a drink of water and a handful of grain.

He cleaned the pup and fed it before returning it to the knapsack. The Queen turned her head to smell the little traveler on her back. This time she didn't snort. The pup was already asleep.

James had seen something special in the little pup. The dog appeared to be a Saluki, an ancient and noble breed native to Egypt. Salukis were fearless hunters, valued for their blinding speed.

James wrote the word, 'Saluki,' in the dust. Mary looked at the word and nodded. Then he wrote, 'Suki,' and she smiled. That became the name of their little traveler.

They stopped again, this time at the livestock business so that James could see Elias. The pens and great barn were almost empty. A young man tended the few animals that remained.

James went to the house and found Elias in bed. He greeted the boy with a smile. "I told the Lord he would have to wait to get old Elias until I had seen you one more time. He's getting impatient with me."

The old gentleman raised his hands and James took them and squeezed them with affection. He took a seat beside the bed.

James picked up a tablet that Elias used for calculations and began to write. An hour passed, with Elias reading and commenting. As the story of the past year unfolded, a look of wonder came over the old merchant's face.

"Is she waiting for you, the mother of the Christ?" He asked.

James nodded.

Elias continued, "I'm growing weary. We mustn't either of us keep God waiting any longer. It's time for you to go, and time for me to sleep. Come, let me bless you."

James knelt beside the bed, and Elias placed his hands on the boy's shoulders and prayed:

"May the Lord bless you and keep you: May the Lord make his face to shine upon you, and be gracious to you. May the Lord lift up his countenance upon you and give you peace. Amen."

Elias lay back onto his pillows. "Go now. You have your journey and I have mine."

. . .

James and Mary returned to the road and arrived at Jerusalem before nightfall. The next morning, arrangements were made to join a group of temple worshippers returning to Galilee.

. . .

On that same morning Elias summoned Ezra the scribe to his bedroom. Documents were prepared that made James Daniel his adopted son and legal heir. The land, house, great barn, and yard with its holding pens would pass to the boy upon the death of the kind Elias.

James had come to Elias as a "born in the house" slave, orphaned and mute. Now, he would become the proprietor of the livestock business on the busy Hebron road south of Jerusalem. The thought of it gave the old merchant great pleasure.

James knew nothing of this as he, Mary, and Suki (in the knapsack on the Queen's back), started for Nazareth.

The little Saluki pup, saved from Gehenna, would be with James at the first Christmas.

Chapter 15
John

In the hill country of Judea the angel Gabriel's message to Zacharias was fulfilled. A son was born to Elizabeth in her old age.

On the eighth day family, friends and the curious came for the ritual of circumcision and the naming of the child. Most speculated that the boy would be named Zacharias, after his father.

Elizabeth tried to end the speculation by announcing firmly that the baby's name would be John. A murmur went up from the onlookers. That was against tradition. No one in the Zacharias family had the name John. Surely Elizabeth had misunderstood the wishes of the father.

They turned to Zacharias.

Zacharias called for a writing tablet. He printed the name of the baby on the tablet and held it up for all to see.

Then he startled everyone by saying, "His name is John!"

A floodgate was opened. Zacharias, who had been silent since the angel's appearance in the temple, began to speak. He explained excitedly how the miracle of John's birth signaled the coming of the promised Christ:

"Give thanks to God. The redemption promised to our fathers is at hand. Our redeemer is coming from

the house of David to rescue his people from the enemy."

He held up baby John and said:

"And you, child, will be called the prophet of the most high: you will go before the Lord to prepare his ways, to give knowledge of salvation to his people by the remission of their sins."

The baby's name and birth were considered most unusual by the people of Hebron. But then, nothing about John's life would ever be called usual.

He grew to manhood preferring the desolate countryside to the company of people. He preferred an austere diet that included locusts and wild honey to banqueting and strong wines. He listened for God's voice and seemed to hear it best when alone beneath the canopy of heaven.

At age 30, he would leave the hill country and travel to the Jordan River outside of Jerusalem. Throngs of people would come to hear the message he had learned in solitude:

Prepare the way of the Lord in the wilderness. Make a straight highway for our God in the desert. Every valley will be lifted up, and every mountain and hill will be leveled. The uneven ground will become smooth and the rough places, a plain.

And the glory of the Lord will appear. And all humanity together will see it for the mouth of the Lord has spoken.

Chapter 16
Suki's Adventure

The group of travelers expected to cover 20 miles a day with fair weather and kind providence. The caravan was experiencing both. James and Mary would be in Nazareth in four days.

A steady supply of food worked an amazing change in the malnourished Suki. James put the pup down for longer and longer periods of time, until it simply refused to stay in the knapsack. Suki became a lively pup, running out of the caravan into the open country. The little dog chased everything (but was too small to catch anything).

At night the young dog always found James and slept at his feet. Salukis usually gave loyalty to only one, and obeyed only one voice. Suki chose to belong to James, the one who had saved him from Gehenna.

The caravan encamped the first night at Bethel. It stopped the second at Shechem. The third encampment was planned for Beth Shean, the gateway to the Valley of Jezreel.

It was on the third day, half way to Beth Shean and Jezreel, that Suki had his grand adventure. The dog ran ahead of the caravan, up and over a hilly rise. The pup charged down the other side toward a stand of sycamore trees.

A solitary male Oryx was asleep in a hollowed out depression beneath the trees. The clatter of sand and pebbles kicked up by the dog awakened the antelope. It sprang out of the shadows and charged toward Suki.

The mature animal weighed nearly two hundred pounds, and was 3 feet tall at the shoulder. The horns of the Oryx were nearly 36 inches of tapered violence.

The frightened dog turned and ran frantically back toward the caravan. The larger, faster Oryx rushed after the pup and quickly closed the distance. The throaty bark of the Saluki pup alerted the travelers.

One of the men grabbed his bow and James took out his sling. The two ran up the road and peered over the rise. They saw a racing Suki about to be caught and gored by the angry antelope.

James stepped up to the top of the hill and quickly sent a stone flying in the direction of the Oryx. The round stone struck the ground and ricocheted up into the charging beast. The bouncing rock did little damage; however, it did cause the startled animal to make a fatal mistake.

The rushing animal veered directly into the path of the bowman, giving him a clear target. The arrow flew straight to the mark and struck the Oryx just below the shoulder, delivering a mortal wound. The animal continued for a few yards and then tumbled to the ground and lay still in death.

Suki continued up the rise with ears flapping and legs sending bursts of sand down the hill. The dog circled around James and spied the fallen Oryx. Without breaking stride, Suki rushed back down the hill toward the fallen antelope. The pup circled round and round the Oryx woofing loudly in triumph.

. . .

That night the travelers gathered at a communal fire to enjoy an unexpected and tasty meal of roasted antelope. The caravan leader cut the first piece, a meaty rib, and brought it over to James and Suki.

The man looked at James and then at Suki. When James nodded, the leader dropped the rib in front of the pup. Suki remained still, muscles tensing beneath its tricolored fur.

The dog watched James who again nodded approval, this time to his pup. Suki pounced on the rib and carried it off into the night. The travelers laughed and clapped their hands in appreciation of the little dog that had made the evening possible.

Chapter 17
Nazareth

The next morning, the fourth morning of travel, the caravan awoke to a cloudless sky. Several came to say goodbye to Mary and James, and to bide them Godspeed.

Mary graciously received her fellow travelers, but James and Suki were already busy packing for the journey. James wondered what might happen to Mary when the people of Nazareth learned she was expecting a child.

The caravan continued north while Mary and James turned westward, into the valley of Jezreel. The wide plain was a waving sea of barley ready for harvest.

A few fields of wheat were interspersed with the barley. It would be another month before the wheat ripened for harvest. That was one of the reasons why most of the fields were barley. It ripened earlier and withstood disease better than wheat. Barley also survived in storage better than wheat.

The Jezreel road stayed south of Mount Moreh. Then it turned northwestward and climbed out of the plain into the hill country of Nazareth.

Mary was quiet. She was praying as they neared her village. James wanted to give Mary a verse he had memorized:

You are my hiding place. You will protect me from trouble and surround me with songs of deliverance.

But he only had his silence to give. He rode closer to her, as if to share her burden.

They topped a rise and saw the village. Nazareth was on a saucer shaped bit of land flanked by terraced hills. It was a ten acre cluster of thatched homes. Mary's home was one of these.

All the homes in Nazareth were similar in appearance. They were constructed of large stacked stones held in place by smaller stones. Mud and straw were used for mortar and covering. Most houses contained four rooms.

The floors were made of pounded dirt. There were stone storage areas in the floors for grains and other foods. Many homes also had plastered stone cisterns for water. Ceilings were constructed of wood beams with insulation of straw caked mud for protection against cold and heat.

The homes were spaced so that families could have a barn and yard for animals. A trickle of water ran through the village from a well on a nearby hill. Most of the families had garden plots because of the water.

The people of Nazareth were farmers. The terrain and climate produced a variety of foods. It was especially adapted for grapes. The vines yielded grapes in season and raisins out of season. The villagers drank wine from the grapes and milk from the goats and sheep.

Figs trees were numerous in the village and countryside providing shade and firewood. The fruit could be harvested twice a year, with the latter being the more abundant harvest. The figs were dried and stored for consumption during the lean winter months.

Clusters of olive trees also dotted the village. The olives were harvested and crushed for oil. The oil was used for lamps, cooking and medicines. Small plots of alluvial soil grew an abundance of barley and wheat for bread. Bread was the main staple of every meal.

Four miles north of Nazareth was Zippori, a major city of Israel. It was a source of employment for craftsmen like Joseph, to whom Mary was betrothed.

Mary's family warmly received James and thanked him for helping Mary. He acknowledged their gratitude, and then left the home to lead the donkeys across the yard to the barn.

Suki raced about the barn, sniffing the floor and corners. He cautiously approached the sheep and goats which were bedded down for the night. The sleepy animals were indifferent to the little dog.

The journey had taught Suki to keep silent around other animals. It was a painful lesson. Donkeys had kicked at him and nipped him. He had been peppered with stones from travelers irritated by his throaty barking. He ran to James but received no sympathy from his young master. The barking ceased around the caravan animals.

James put the saddle packs in the storage room of the barn. He made his bed in it, just as he had done in the barn of Elias, and also of Aaron and Rachel.

It would be his home for the next six months.

The open front of the barn allowed the evening breeze to circulate into the room. But there was no window in the room showing off the night sky.

A large sycamore fig tree grew midway between the house and barn. James sometimes climbed the tree after supper to gaze at the village and surrounding hills. He would stay there to watch the stars begin to appear.

He was in the tree the evening Mary told Joseph about the coming of the first Christmas.

Chapter 18
Mary and Joseph

There was a bench beneath the sycamore tree that Joseph had made for Mary. He had put it under the tree so that the two of them would have a private place to sit and talk. The bench was in view of the house. This made its use by the couple acceptable to Mary's family.

James was sitting in the tree after supper when Mary and Joseph came out of the house. They turned away from the path leading to the yard gate and came to the tree. Mary sat on the bench while Joseph stood looking down at her.

"I have so much to tell you," Mary said. "Please listen to all before you speak."

Joseph smiled down at the young woman who was to be his wife.

"Three months ago an angel of the Lord appeared to me," Mary began.

Joseph stopped smiling.

"I was frightened. The angel assured me that in the eyes of the Lord I was favored and blessed among all women. I wasn't to be afraid."

"I'm going to have a son, and he is to be called Jesus. He will be the promised Christ, who will be a king and sit on the throne of David. He will rule over God's people forever and there will be no end to his kingdom."

Joseph sat down.

Mary continued: "I couldn't understand how this was possible, since I've never known any man. The angel said it would happen to me through the power of God's Spirit. The child that will be born to me shall be called the son of God."

"Then the angel told me that my aged cousin, Elizabeth, was expecting a child. Nothing is impossible with God. The angel waited for my response."

"I answered from my heart. 'I am the handmaid of the Lord. Let it be to me as you have said.'"

Joseph leaned away from Mary.

"I left Nazareth to be with Elizabeth. The visit confirmed all that the angel had told me. The child of Elizabeth and Zacharias is the one who will proclaim the coming of the Christ. And the child I carry within me is that promised Christ of our people."

Joseph had kept his silence. Now he stared into the gathering evening, seeing but not seeing. Suddenly he stood up, his face a mask of sadness. He crossed the yard to the gate and disappeared down the path toward his home.

Mary bowed her head. Was she weeping, James wondered? Then, he heard her voice. She was singing softly,

"Great is the Lord.
My spirit rejoices in God my Savior."

It was a song he had first heard in the home of Elizabeth and Zacharias. He had heard it on the journey to Nazareth. He had matched a tune to the words. He would play for her as she sang. This had pleased her. The song continued,

> *"He has favored His humble daughter.*
> *I will be called blessed, from generation to*
> *generation."*

James began to play his reed pipe. Mary stopped singing and looked up into the branches. Then she took up the song again:

> *"The Mighty One,*
> *His name is holy.*
>
> *He has done great things.*
> *He has shown mercy to those who fear Him.*
>
> *He has scattered the proud, and toppled the mighty.*
> *He has exalted the lowly, and satisfied the hungry.*
>
> *He has helped Israel with mercy.*
> *He is faithful to our fathers forever and forever."*

The music of voice and reed pipe died away. Silence like a warm cloak settled over house, yard, and barn. In the stillness James sensed a heavenly peace surrounding the young woman beneath the tree.

Mary rose and without looking up, said, "Goodnight. God give you rest," and walked to the house.

. . .

Joseph continued toward his home, wrestling with the undeniable. Mary was carrying a child and the child was not his. The betrothal would have to be broken.

70

Joseph was a good and kind man. He could not (and would not) act meanly toward Mary and her family because of this unhappy circumstance. He decided to break the betrothal privately. That would spare Mary and the family the humiliation of a public divorce.

He would tell them of his decision the following evening. With the matter settled in his mind he retired for the night. The following evening he called at Mary's home again. What he told the family astonished all but Mary.

"I had decided to break the betrothal privately to spare you as much pain as possible," Joseph said. "That was my resolve as I finally fell into a troubled sleep. As I slept, an angel appeared to me more real than any waking experience!"

"The angel said:

'Joseph, son of David, don't be afraid to take Mary as your wife, because what has been conceived in her is by the Holy Spirit. She will give birth to a son, and you are to name him Jesus, because he will save his people from their sins.'"

Joseph paused and gathered himself. What he was about to say would be the most important thing he would ever say.

"Mary, God has chosen me to care for you and the precious gift you carry. Will you trust me to do this?"

Thus, the young woman and her unborn baby were given into the hands of this strong man. Mary lived quietly and privately during the remaining months of her pregnancy. Joseph carefully shielded her from public suspicion and gossip.

Whenever Joseph's work in Zippori required four hands rather than two, he took James with him to the work site. He patiently taught James how to work with wood and stone.

James learned other lessons by observing Joseph.

An employer might become irate. Joseph never raised his voice. He gave more than a measure of work for a measure of pay. He kept his word and asked the same of others, no more and no less.

He never left for tomorrow what could be accomplished today. James thought that was the reason Joseph napped so easily after noon lunch.

Joseph offered James only one piece of advice, and that was after another boy had mocked his silence. He said to James, "Don't do to others what you would not want others to do to you."

James had been in Nazareth for six months when Joseph decided to leave.

A decree of the Roman emperor required every person of the empire to register in the town or city of family origin. Bethlehem had been the boyhood home of King David. Joseph was a descendent of the king.

It was Joseph's decision to take Mary with him to Bethlehem to register for the census. They would remain there, even after the birth of the baby. In a strange city, many miles from Nazareth, there would be no prying questions or accusatory looks.

It was a one day's journey from Bethlehem on to the hill country of Hebron. James would accompany Joseph and Mary and then travel on to his home.

Joseph's decision meant that Bethlehem, not Nazareth, would be the scene of the first Christmas, just as the Holy Scriptures had prophesied: *"But you, Bethlehem Ephratah..."*

It also meant that James, The Queen, and Suki would be present at the first Christmas.

Chapter 19
Bethlehem

Bethlehem was approximately seven miles south of Jerusalem. The humble white stone homes were built upon a limestone ridge just above the road to Hebron and Egypt. It was overflowing with travelers when Joseph, Mary, and James arrived.

Joseph inquired about lodgings and was pointed to one of the larger houses in the village. Mary's time was close. The inn of Bethlehem was a stone house of several rooms. There was a natural limestone cave beneath the inn. It had been enlarged to serve as a barn.

An enclosure in front of the cave provided a spacious yard for the animals of those staying at the inn. There were lean-tos against the outside of the fence. These provided additional overnight shelter when the inn was crowded.

Joseph asked for lodgings, but the innkeeper just shook his head. Every available space in the inn was occupied, even the lean-tos.

The man studied the weary couple, especially the young woman. "The barn beneath the inn is warm and dry," he said. "Perhaps you could use it?"

"Yes," said Joseph. "Thank you. We will take it."

The innkeeper again looked at Mary. His voice softened. "There is a room at the back of the cave. It's not large. You can move things out to make room for her. It can be made private."

He disappeared into the inn and returned with a rectangular covering. "Hang this at the entrance to the room. There are hooks in the ceiling."

Joseph helped Mary onto The Queen's back and walked beside her, holding Mary as James led the donkey down the path to the yard and cave entrance. Mary and Joseph entered the barn, while James and Suki returned up the path. James brought down the other donkey and supplies into the enclosure.

The many travelers handled the overcrowding of the inn with a good-natured acceptance. Cooking fires started up in front of the lean-tos. Travelers moved in and out of the barn. They carried straw for the animals and bedding for themselves.

They talked and laughed and complained loudly about the tyrant in Rome who had put them to this trouble. Animals were fed and watered and tethered inside the fence next to their owner's lean-tos.

Other livestock milled about in the open yard. The innkeeper's sheep and goats had already been penned up for the night inside the cave.

The hum of activity subsided after the evening meal was finished and the fires were extinguished. Travelers and livestock became quiet. None seemed curious about the woman in the cave behind the curtain.

James put The Queen and the other donkey in an empty stall, just inside the barn. He spread his bed against the stall. Propped against it, he would be able to watch the night sky.

Mary served them a cold supper of cheese, bread and figs. She moved slowly, pausing at times in obvious pain. Joseph and James hurriedly cleared the room and made a bed for her.

Joseph found an empty feed trough, and he and James brought it to the room. Next, he added straw and covered it with a woolen saddle blanket. The rough stone manger was now a cradle.

James and Suki left the room and went to see to the donkeys. He fed them and put out fresh straw and water. He brushed their coats and cleaned their hooves. Then he settled onto his bed and leaned against the stall wall. Stars began to light the sky. Suki walked round and round in the fresh straw and finally lay down at his feet.

The curtain closed on the room at the back of the cave. Only the angels of heaven would be witnesses to the birth of the first Christmas.

Chapter 20
First Christmas

Soft, low sounds came from the back of the barn, awakening James. Joseph came out of the room and filled a pitcher with water. He returned to the room at the rear of the cave, closing the curtain. Light came from beneath the curtain.

The Queen was also awake. She had come to the front of the stall and was looking into the night. Her ears were up, as though she were listening to something (or for something).

James stood at the entrance to the cave. The yard and the inn were silent. The distant sky glowed with a strange light. The light seemed to undulate from the clouds to the earth.

The cry of a baby came from the little room. Joseph was rubbing the infant with a mixture of salt and oil. He then bathed and dried the little body before placing the baby in Mary's arms.

"He will be called Jesus," Joseph said.

Mary wrapped her little son in swaddling strips against the night air. She cradled him to her breast. The notes of a reed pipe floated back to the little room. Mary began to sing sweetly to the newborn.

"God gives sleep my little one.
Now steals upon my sleepy one.
Sleep on, sleep on, and sleep on.

Go to sleep, my little one.
Sleepy eyes close, my little one.
Sleep on, sleep on, and sleep on.

Angels watch o'er my little one,
Love enfolds my little one.
Sleep on, sleep on, and sleep on.

Go to sleep, my little one.
Sleepy eyes close, my little one.
Sleep on, sleep on, and sleep on."

As James put his reed pipe away, Joseph gently took the sleeping baby from Mary's arms. She closed her eyes and slipped into an exhausted sleep.

Joseph came from behind the curtain carrying the newborn. "Light a lamp. I want you to see God's little son," he said to James.

James lit the lamp in the holder by the cave entrance. The Queen peered over the stall at Joseph and the baby. Suki looked from Joseph to James, and then back to Joseph and the bundle in his arms.

Joseph placed the infant in the boy's arms. James gazed down into the tiny sleeping face. The swaddling clothes were snug about his little form. James lifted the child and placed a kiss on his warm cheek.

He thought of a verse from Aaron's Isaiah scroll that spoke of this moment: "Prince of Peace."

The voice startled James. Joseph was looking at him. He too, had heard the voice. The Queen and Suki were looking at him. They had heard the voice. James looked about the barn to see who had spoken. No one was there. And then he knew!

Something was also happening to his face. Joseph was smiling at him and James was smiling back. He smiled down at the bundle he cradled in his arm.

"Little Prince of Peace," James said again.

He looked at The Queen. "Queenie," he said. The Queen stretched her head toward James and he rubbed her soft nose. She sniffed the baby. Her erect ears relaxed and she lowered her proud head.

James looked down at the half-grown puppy. "Suki," he said. The dog stretched itself up to James so that he could rub his long, soft ears. Suki looked up at the baby in his master's arm and dropped down to rest at James' feet, muzzle between paws.

Joseph took the baby and returned to the room. He gently placed the sleeping infant in the manger. He too, closed his eyes and slept. The white glow in the distant sky had faded away. The Queen had retreated back into her stall and was asleep.

Suki hadn't waited for James. The dog was curled up asleep at the edge of the wool mat. James sat down and leaned his head back. He closed his eyes and he too, slept.

The first Christmas had touched James Daniel and he was forever changed.

Chapter 21
Shepherds

There were stirrings in the early morning darkness at the inn and in the lean-tos against the fence. Bethlehem was waking up. That was when the shepherds arrived in the yard. They milled about, whispering to one another.

James stood in the entrance of the cave and watched them. When the men saw James they moved toward him. Their dress told him that they were shepherds. One of the men stepped forward and James recognized him. It was Eliphaz from the Hebron road adventure.

"We are seeking a baby lying in a manger," Eliphaz explained. "That is why we have come to this barn."

He paused and studied James. The boy was taller, but the same boy.

"It is you!" he exclaimed. "You are the young David who stopped our mischief on the Hebron road." He touched the scar on the bridge of his nose. "My brothers are with me."

Bildad and Zophar appeared, one on each side of Eliphaz.

"We mean no harm," Eliphaz continued. "We are shepherds doing honest work. How is the good priest who put us back on the side of God?"

"I believe he's well," James replied. "The baby you seek is here. How did you know about the child?"

All three brothers began to speak. "The angel of the Lord told us he is the promised Christ. He's lying in a manger. The child is here in the city of David. The angel said it was so."

"We were afraid," they continued. "There was a great light. It was in the clouds and all around us. Then there were many angels. They were in the clouds, too."

"The angels sang, '*Glory to God in the highest, and on earth peace, good will toward men.*' Then we were not afraid."

Joseph had come to stand beside James. "The baby you seek is here. He's asleep. Come and see."

The three brothers and the other shepherds meekly followed Joseph and James into the cave. Bildad stopped to look at The Queen. She withdrew into the darkened stall.

Bildad looked at the shadowy figure at the back of the stall. He rubbed his chin. "We both remember," he said.

Joseph took down the curtain. Mary was seated holding the baby. The men entered the room awkwardly. They were common laborers, ordinary and unassuming men at the bottom of life's ladder.

Mary removed the swaddling clothes from her little son and placed the baby in the manger.

The men crowded around. The newborn, free of the swaddling clothes, stretched tiny arms and legs.

The shepherds gave a collective, "Ah."

The three brothers knelt by the stone manger. The other shepherds followed the example of Eliphaz,

Zophar and Bildad. They gazed back and forth from baby, to young mother, to baby.

It was Eliphaz who finally spoke to Mary:

"We were in the fields keeping watch over our flocks. The clouds lit up with a heavenly light that shined down all around us. The angel of the Lord appeared and told us not to be afraid. We were told of the birth of your son in the city of David. The angel said your baby is a Savior who is Christ the Lord."

Mary bowed her head to the elder brother.

"The baby's name is Jesus," Joseph said. "It means he will save his people from their sins."

Again there was a collective, "Ah."

"The angel told us to seek out a baby wrapped in swaddling clothes lying in a manger," Eliphaz said, and he was done.

There was a comfortable silence as the humble men watched the family.

One of the men thought it would be good to pray. They murmured in agreement. One of them touched the shoulder of Eliphaz. "Eliphaz you do it."

Eliphaz froze, panic on his face.

Joseph saw it and turned to James. "James we have never heard you pray aloud. Will you pray?"

James Daniel bowed his head. A rush of God's love suffused him. An emotional wall melted away and warm tears moistened his cheeks. He who could not speak was now to pray in the presence of God's son.

He heard Aaron's voice reading from the Isaiah scroll. He saw the words on his limestone tablet. He began to pray.

"For to us a child is born, to us a son is given: and the government shall be upon his shoulders. And his name shall be called Wonderful Counsellor, Mighty God, Everlasting Father, Prince of Peace."

He finished his prayer. "Amen."

In unison the brothers and shepherds said, "Amen."

The shepherds stood up and filed out of the room and into the yard. Men, women and children were standing about, watching the cave.

The men excitedly told of what they had seen and heard. They left the inn and returned to the flocks, glorifying and praising God.

. . .

That morning, Joseph left the cave and the inn and disappeared into Bethlehem. When he returned he had food, wine, milk, and good news.

"I've found a house. It's at the edge of the village. It has no barn, but James and I will build one."

Chapter 22
Consecration

When Mary was strong enough, the family moved into the house. Joseph and James started to construct the barn immediately.

James remained with the family for eight days until the ritual of circumcision. The 2000-year-old rite dated back to the time of Abraham. It took place in the morning, as had become the custom of the Jewish people.

The ceremony was attended by a small gathering that included the innkeeper; a few travelers who were at the inn that wondrous night, and some of the shepherds. The three brothers were among the shepherds and were led into the small house by Eliphaz. All of the shepherds sat with downcast eyes and bowed heads.

The Rabbi who was to perform the circumcision was as poor as the people of Bethlehem that he served. He was also a man of humble spirit who fully grasped the importance of the ritual he was to complete. The God of the universe had chosen Israel to be his people.

Quoting from the sacred scriptures, his voice strained with emotion, the Rabbi said:

"Every male among you shall be circumcised. And you shall be circumcised in the flesh of your foreskin, and it shall be a token of a covenant between me and you. And he that is eight days old shall be circumcised among you, every male throughout your generations."

The Rabbi paused after completing the circumcision, his head bowed in respectful awe before the God of Israel. He then passed the infant Jesus into the hands of Joseph.

Joseph held the baby boy up to heaven and prayed an ancient prayer of dedication in which the child is named:

"Our God and God of our fathers sustain this child for his father and mother and let his name in Israel be Jesus, son of Joseph. Amen."

After the prayer, Eliphaz raised his head and turned to the assembled guests, "It means he will save his people from their sins," he said knowingly. The heads of Zophar and Bildad nodded vigorously in agreement.

Mary served a small feast to her guests. The brothers especially enjoyed the meal, staying until the last morsel was eaten.

. . .

That evening, with the new barn finished, James told Mary and Joseph that he would leave for the hill country of Hebron at dawn.

"Of course," Joseph said. "It's right for you to return to your home."

Mary kissed the boy's cheek. "Promise us that you will come back?" she asked hopefully. James nodded.

. . .

When the 33 days of Mary's purification had elapsed, the couple carried the little Christ to the temple in Jerusalem for his consecration.

As it is written in the law of the Lord, Every male that opens the womb shall be called holy to the Lord.

Joseph purchased two turtle doves (the offering of the poor) that would be given for burnt offering and sacrifice.

Unknown to the little family, two saints were waiting for them in the temple court. One was Anna, a holy widow of 84 years, who prayed in the temple day and night. The other was an aged man named Simeon.

God had promised Simeon that he would see Israel's Messiah before he saw death. Now Simeon was in the temple at the precise moment that Joseph, Mary, and the infant Jesus entered.

First Simeon, and then Anna, came up to Mary and the infant. They raised their voices to bless the little family. Then each of them held the baby and gave thanks, praising God the Father for Israel's redemption.

People stopped what they were doing and listened to the words of Simeon and Anna. A crowd gathered about the humble couple to gaze upon Mary's baby.

The temple experience was another precious memory that Mary treasured up in her heart.

As soon as the consecration was completed, Joseph and Mary, with God's little son, quietly slipped out of the temple and back into obscurity.

Chapter 23
Little Mother

James slipped quietly into the yard and led The Queen to the barn. He watered and fed her, and then he put her into the stall with the little Prince who was asleep in the straw. She nuzzled the colt awake. The yearling sprang up excitedly. He looked like The Queen, with his four white fetlocks and reddish brown coat.

Ahab came to the stall divide and put his head over to welcome her. She moved near him and patiently accepted his nuzzles.

The saddle packs were stowed in the little room with the window. James put fresh straw on the floor and rolled out his bed. Suki circled and tromped the straw until he was satisfied with it. Then he lay down at the end of the woolen mat.

James crossed the yard to the limestone house. Aaron opened the door at his knock. The light shone from behind him onto the face of the tall, slim boy.

"James Daniel! Rachel, it's the boy. He's come home." He pulled James into the room. Rachel stood with her hands clasped together.

James crossed to her and took her clasped hands in his. He bent and kissed her softly on the cheek.

"Little mother," he said gently. Henceforth, that would be the term of endearment he used when addressing Rachel.

At the sound of his voice, Rachel's hands flew to her mouth. Then she was joyfully hugging him. Aaron joined the happiness.

He guided James to the table. "Sit down. You must be tired. What has happened? Tell us everything."

"You must be hungry," Rachel said. She began to gather food for the table.

James tried not to leave out anything as he told them of the past six months. He dwelt on the story of Bethlehem and the birth of the Christ child. He told of kissing the baby and the miracle of finding his voice.

"And what has happened here since I've been away?" James inquired.

Aaron put his hands together and cleared his throat. "I have unhappy news. Elias has been gathered to the bosom of Abraham. Zacharias and I were with him at the end. His final thoughts were of you."

James became still. His stoic defense against painful emotions was gone. It had evaporated with the kiss on the baby's cheek. Now he was overwhelmed with grief at the loss of this dear old man who had been so kind to him.

Rachel came beside him, putting her arms around him and her cheek on his head. She said nothing, she just held him. James felt the pain in his heart begin to ease. This was all very new to the boy. He had never experienced the comfort of one human being to another.

After a time, Aaron continued. "Zacharias and Elizabeth have a healthy son. His name is John. He's almost too much for them. Zacharias says he and Elizabeth are too old to be parents. They are more like grandparents."

"They may indulge him and let him have his way. That's not altogether a bad thing if it's also God's way."

"Jema sends you a message," Rachel added. "She said to tell you that you may come for your tablet. Do you know what that means?"

"Yes," said James, "I think I know what it means."

Then she said, "I'll fix a bed for you in the house tonight."

"No, little mother. I will spend one last night in the barn. I have a dog with me. We will learn about houses together tomorrow night."

James returned to the barn and watched the stars from his bed of straw. He thought of Jema. Would she be glad to see him? Is that what her message meant? He had changed. Had she? Tomorrow he would...and he was asleep.

Though Jema had not been with James, the first Christmas was about to come to her.

Chapter 24
Jema

Jema was seated on her favorite rock. It was the one on which she had carved her name. She was changed. The young girl had matured into a young maiden.

"I've come for my tablet," said a voice behind her.

She turned and looked back. Her face flushed with astonished happiness. "James, you can speak! How wonderful for you. Yes, I have your tablet," she exclaimed.

Jema watched the tall figure coming near. James the boy had disappeared. He was being replaced by a youth on the way to becoming a man.

"You have it here?" James asked.

"Of course," she replied. "You asked me to keep it for you. I have it with me always."

James sat on the rock beside her. Jema reached into her knapsack and withdrew the tablet. His message was erased, and she had printed, "James Daniel."

James slipped the tablet into his knapsack. The young maiden on the rock also slipped into his heart. She replaced the girl he had regarded with boyish awe.

"I was there in Bethlehem when Mary's baby was born," he said. "Her little son is the Christ; the Savior that God promised he would send."

His voice softened, "I held him in my arms. Jema, I kissed his cheek; and in that moment God made me whole and gave me a voice."

Jema studied his face with her dark eyes. "You kissed the child of God?" she asked in wonder.

During the many months Jema and James had sat together, lunched together, and driven the sheep and goats together, they had never touched.

Jema raised her fingers and lightly touched his lips. A shudder went through her. Instead of withdrawing her hand, her fingers pressed more firmly, involuntarily against his mouth. She sighed and leaned into him for support. He held her and felt her trembling. It lasted for only a moment, and then she pulled away.

Her eyes were closed. She seemed unaware of where she was or that James was seated beside her. James waited, unsure of what to say or do. And then her eyes opened and she was back.

She gave him a sweet smile. "Walk and talk with me while I move the goats to water," she said. "I want to hear your voice-hear all about what has happened."

Jema picked up her walking stick, stood up, and fitted it beneath her arm. James, still seated, looked at her exposed feet.

"Sit down, Jema," he instructed her gently. She looked at him questioningly. "Please sit down," he repeated.

She did as he asked. He knelt before her and put his hand around her foot. When he touched her foot she tried to withdraw it, but he held on to it firmly. Jema relaxed, trusting him. He began to unwrap the cloth binding.

"No," Jema said, and again tried to draw the foot under the covering of her dress. "You mustn't," she said and turned away. James gently held the foot and continued to unwrap it, laying the cloth strips on the rock. Then he held the small foot on his palm, staring at it. Jema withdraw it and moved it beneath the dress. He sat down again beside her.

Jema stared at the hem of her dress and then lifted it slowly. She looked down at the exposed foot. She gasped and dropped the dress around it. She remained still, with her head bowed, looking down at the ground.

Again Jema lifted the hem away from her small foot, this time tentatively lowering it to the ground. She stared at her foot and then dropped and smoothed the dress around it.

She pressed the foot into the earth several times. Then Jema put a hand on James' shoulder and stood up. She looked down at him, her faced bathed in a smile of pure joy. She extended her arms for balance and took two steps away from the rock. Then, with more confidence, she slowly turned round and round, flaring out the hem of her dress.

Jema stopped in front of James and put her hands on his shoulders. She leaned close to his ear. Her voice was thick with emotion as she whispered; "James, you came back. And you brought me this gift from the child of God!"

Jema walked away from James, pulling the covering from her head to expose her glorious black hair. She turned her face to the sun

With strong melodious voice, Jema sang out to heaven, "Hosanna!" The word traveled down the valley and crashed against the hillside rocks echoing back, "Hosanna...Hosanna." She laughed and shouted again, "Hosanna!" And again the rocks and valley answered back.

And then Jema, who had never danced, danced in joyous ecstasy.

Chapter 25
Jemania Inn

James traveled with Aaron and Zacharias each time they came to Jerusalem to serve in the temple. He spent the remainder of the days on his property, repairing the buildings that had been neglected. He re-thatched the roofs of the house and barn. Stone walls in both were repaired and sealed. Fences were mended.

After a year, he and Suki moved into the house. James reopened the livestock business to considerable success. He credited this to the reputation of the good Elias. Customers soon recognized the same qualities of truthfulness and fair dealing in the young proprietor.

James kept his word to Mary about returning to Bethlehem. He, Suki and The Queen went to Bethlehem periodically to visit his friends and little Jesus. These visits became less frequent as he continued to develop his property.

The following year, James started a second business by enlarging the house and turning the over-sized building into an inn. He called it the Jemania Inn. The demands of the new business made trips to Bethlehem less frequent.

James also constructed three large sheds, each with double doors that opened out toward the Hebron road. These were leased to a blacksmith, a harness maker and a feed merchant.

Now James could provide almost everything travelers might need. The businesses prospered and the inn became a preferred stop on the Jerusalem-Hebron road.

One evening, well into the night, a knock summoned James to the door. He opened the door cautiously; it was much too late for normal travelers. The light from the room shone on the exhausted face of Joseph.

"We are so thankful to be standing at your door," he said. James looked past Joseph to Mary, who was leaning wearily against the donkey and holding her small son on the light saddle pack.

James was delighted to see them; but he was concerned by their appearance. He wondered: were they rushing to something, or fleeing from something to look so tired?

James guided them inside the crowded inn and took them to his own room.

Joseph protested. "No James, we can't take your bed."

"You mustn't deny me this act of hospitality to my friends and the little Christ," James said. "I'll sleep in the barn and be better for it."

Despite the lateness of the hour, he also insisted that they dine with him.

After the meal, the little boy fed Suki with the table scraps. Joseph remained at the table while Mary and Jesus followed James to his room, the only room and bed available in the inn.

Joseph chose to stay behind to tell James an amazing story: a tale of Magi from the east, a miraculous star, and a mad king bent on murder.

Suki would have followed the little boy to the room but James retrieved the dog and led it back to the dining table.

Chapter 26
Flight to Egypt

"Some of what I am going to tell you is firsthand knowledge," Joseph began. "Some of it I know from others. And some of it I know because God revealed it to me."

Suki lay down at the feet of James as Joseph continued.

"A caravan of wealthy, learned men traveling from the east came to Jerusalem. How long they had traveled or how far they had come isn't known."

"They had seen a new star. To them it was a sign that the promised Messiah, the king of the Jews, had been born. The star was not fixed, but moved. It led them to Jerusalem."

"Did they speak to King Herod?" James asked.

"Yes," said Joseph. "Herod pretended to welcome the Magi and the news of the birth of a heaven-sent king. His real intention was to murder the child, to murder our little son."

"What did Herod do?" James asked.

"He called the priests and the scribes together to ask what they knew about the birth of a king," Joseph answered. "They told the king that Bethlehem was prophesied as the birthplace of this king."

Joseph continued, "He encouraged the men from the east to continue their quest in Bethlehem. He asked that they bring him word if they found the child, so that he might worship the newborn king."

"He's an old fox," James said.

"He's worse," said Joseph. "He is evil itself."

Then Joseph returned to the subject of the Magi. "The star led the wise men to Bethlehem and to our home. You can imagine our surprise when they appeared at our door."

"The men quickly explained the reason for their journey. 'We saw a new star in the heavens,' they said. 'It was the star of a newborn king. The star began to move and we followed it. When the star stopped over this house we were filled with excitement and joy.'"

Joseph continued, "They looked at Mary holding our little son and said; 'We believe we have found the king! Our long journey is ended. Please, may we enter?'"

"The visitors entered our home and gave the child gifts of gold, frankincense and myrrh: gifts for a king. Then, these great men bowed down and worshipped before our little Jesus."

James pictured these wealthy strangers kneeling before Jesus. He also remembered the lowly shepherds kneeling at the stone manger. One day he thought, all of mankind will kneel before this child.

"Early the next morning, I discovered that they had broken camp and were ready to leave. When I asked them why, this is what they told me:

'We were warned by an angel in a dream not to tell Herod that we had found the little king. We were told to return to our home by another way.'"

"They left so suddenly," Joseph said, "that most of Bethlehem was unaware of our unusual guests."

"Was their sudden departure the reason you left your home?" James asked.

"No," Joseph replied, "It was another dream, but perhaps the same angel. The angel of the Lord appeared to me and warned me to take Mary and our child and to flee to Egypt, because King Herod was intent on killing Jesus."

"Tomorrow evening, we will be with Zacharias and Elizabeth in Hebron. After that, we will travel as far as we can each day until our son is safely hidden in Egypt."

"Sleep in peace tonight," James said. "Leave the preparation for the journey to me. After all, that's my business now."

Joseph and James said good night and James went to the barn to make preparations.

The next morning, when Joseph, Mary and the little boy came to the barn, they were surprised to see two donkeys packed and ready for their trip.

Mary went to the second donkey and stroked the proud head of The Queen. She picked up little Jesus and placed him on The Queen's back. The Queen turned her head and looked at the little boy. A ripple of pleasure seemed to go through her when the boy put his small arms around her neck.

"Thank you for The Queen," Mary said warmly. "We will bring her back to you."

Out of an old habit, James simply nodded. Mary smiled and touched his cheek. Then, the little family and The Queen were off to Egypt, far away from the evil king.

Not long after the Magi had left Bethlehem, King Herod realized that his deception had failed. The mad king ordered the murder of all little boys, two years and younger, in and around the village of Bethlehem.

Cruel henchmen of the king carried out the order. Jesus was not among the innocents who were killed. The angel's warning to Joseph had saved God's little son.

The family stayed in Egypt until King Herod was dead. Then an angel of the Lord again spoke to Joseph in a dream saying: "The one who wanted to harm the child is no more. Now you can return."

The little family returned to Israel, and The Queen was gratefully given back to James.

Joseph, Mary, and Jesus, chose not to return to Bethlehem. Instead, they traveled on to Nazareth of Galilee and made their home among family and friends.

Jesus found approval in the eyes of everyone who watched him grow. His Heavenly Father was also pleased with the son he had sent into the world.

Less than a half century later, a writer summed up the first Christmas with just 25 words:

For God so loved the world that he gave his only begotten son, that whoever believes in him should not perish, but have everlasting life.

Epilogue

In the fullness of time, a dark eyed, dark haired young woman came to manage the Jemania Inn for James. Not coincidentally, her name was also Jemania. Her grace and beauty were spoken of from Alexandria to Damascus.

James called the woman, Jema. But of course, that was a husband's privilege.

Travelers observed that a lean and graceful dog named Suki was always at his side. He also kept a donkey in a special stall in the barn. She was called The Queen because of her proud demeanor.

The stall had a double window that could be opened at night to reveal the stars and catch the evening breeze. On some evenings, travelers thought they heard a shepherd's reed pipe and the voice of a woman coming from the open window:

"Rose of Sharon:
Lily of the Valley.
Apple tree among trees:
Apricots ripe with fragrance.

So is my beloved, among the sons.
Under his shadow, I will delight.
Love of my beloved,
Fruit sweet to taste."

The Queen freely wandered about the property. Some guests thought she pranced about much too proudly for a lowly donkey.

She especially liked small children. They would ride on her back around the yard, pulling on her long ears and rubbing her soft nose.

The End

Scriptures not Referenced in the Text

Some scriptures are quoted. Some scriptures are paraphrased. Some scriptures are selectively rephrased for lyrics.

Chapter 4

As a father pities his children, even so God pities them who fear him, for he knows our frame that we are dust.
Psalm 103:13-14

Chapter 5

Take off your shoes. The ground upon which you are standing is holy ground.
Exodus 3:5

Chapter 8

The Lord is our strength and song. And he is become our salvation. He is our God. We will prepare him a habitation, the God of our fathers, and exalt him.
Exodus 15:2

Chapter 11

Your word have I hid in my heart, that I might not sin against you.
Psalm 119:11

Rose of Sharon: Lily of the Valley. Apple tree among trees: Apricots ripe with fragrance. So is my

beloved, among the sons. Under his shadow, I will delight. Love of my beloved, Fruit sweet to taste.
Song of Songs 2:1-3

Chapter 12

Therefore the Lord himself shall give you a sign; behold a virgin shall conceive and bear a son, and shall call his name Immanuel.
Isaiah 7:14

But you, Bethlehem Ephratah, though you are small among thousands of Judah, yet out of you shall come forth to me a ruler in Israel; whose origins are from of old, from everlasting.
Micah 5:2

The heavens are the work of your fingers. The moon and stars you have ordained. O Lord, how excellent is your name in all the earth.

Praise him sun and moon. Praise him all you stars of light. O Lord, how excellent is your name in all the earth.
Psalm 8

Chapter 14

The Lord bless you and keep you. The Lord make his face to shine upon you, and be gracious to you. The Lord lift up his countenance upon you and give you peace. Amen.
Numbers 6:24-26

Chapter 15

Give thanks to God. The redemption promised to our fathers is at hand. Our redeemer is coming from the house of David to rescue his people from the enemy.
Luke 1:68-71

And you, child, will be called the prophet of the most high: for you will go before the Lord to prepare his ways, to give knowledge of salvation to his people by the remission of their sins.
Luke 1:76-77

Prepare the way of the Lord in the wilderness. Make a straight highway for our God in the desert. Every valley will be lifted up, and every mountain and hill will be leveled. The uneven ground will become smooth and the rough places, a plain.

And the glory of the Lord will appear. And all humanity together will see it for the mouth of the Lord has spoken.
Isaiah 40:1-6

Chapter 17

You are my hiding place; you will protect me from trouble and surround me with songs of deliverance.
Psalm 32:7

Chapter 18

Great is the Lord, my spirit rejoices, in God my Savior. He has favored His humble daughter. I will be called blessed, from generation to generation. The Mighty One, His name is holy. He has done great things. He has shown mercy to those who fear Him. He has scattered the proud, and toppled the mighty. He has exalted the lowly, and satisfied the hungry. He has helped Israel with mercy.

He is faithful to our fathers forever and forever.
Luke 1:46-55

Joseph, son of David, don't be afraid to take Mary as your wife, because what has been conceived in her is by the Holy Spirit. She will give birth to a son, and you are to name him Jesus, because he will save his people from their sins.
Matthew 1:20-21

But you, Bethlehem Ephratah
Micah 5:2

Chapter 21

For to us a child is born, to us a son is given: and the government shall be upon his shoulders: and his name shall be called Wonderful Counselor, The Mighty God, The Everlasting Father, The Prince of Peace.
Isaiah 9:6

Chapter 22

Every male among you shall be circumcised. And you shall be circumcised in the flesh of your foreskin, and it shall be a token of a covenant between me and you. And he that is eight days old shall be circumcised among you, every male throughout your generations.
Genesis 17:10-13

As it is written in the law of the Lord, Every male that opens the womb shall be called holy to the Lord.
Luke 2:2322

Chapter 26

For God so loved the world that he gave his only begotten son, that whoever believes in him should not perish, but have everlasting life.
John 3:16

Epilogue

Rose of Sharon: Lily of the Valley. Apple tree among trees: Apricots ripe with fragrance. So is my beloved, among the sons. Under his shadow, I will delight. Love of my beloved, Fruit sweet to taste.
Song of Songs 2:1-3

Also by Wana Archer
Available on Amazon

Advent Edition
James Daniel and the First Christmas

Individuals and families can celebrate the days of Advent and also experience the wonder of the first Christmas through the pages of *James Daniel*.

Complete observances of the four Sundays of Advent, and scripture readings for the days of the Advent calendar, are incorporated into the chapter readings of the book.

THE ANSWER
Solving the Science/Bible Problem

There's a cultural war raging between Secularists and Biblicists over what constitutes truth. This book analyzes the two sides of the controversy. It proposes a solution that honors both the Bible and science.

A clear path to the reconciliation of scientific and biblical truths, free of scientific and theological language, is marked out for the reader to follow.

The place of faith and reason in living the truthful life is explained and offered for the reader's consideration.

Sermons that Change Lives
The Persuasive Sermon

Get ready for a reading experience that will transform your understanding of biblical preaching and teaching. This book offers new insights into the ancient art of proclaiming the Bible.

The book contains 17 model services in the new, effective preaching concept. In addition, the book is a rich source of Bible stories, inspirational illustrations, and humor.

www.ingramcontent.com/pod-product-compliance
Lightning Source LLC
Chambersburg PA
CBHW070636130626

46555CB00006B/2562